Dear Parents and Educators,

Welcome to Penguin Young Readers! As parents and educators, you know that each child develops at his or her own pace—in terms of speech, critical thinking, and, of course, reading. Penguin Young Readers recognizes this fact. As a result, each Penguin Young Readers book is assigned a traditional easy-to-read level (1–4) as well as a Guided Reading Level (A–P). Both of these systems will help you choose the right book for your child. Please refer to the back of each book for specific leveling information. Penguin Young Readers features esteemed authors and illustrators, stories about favorite characters, fascinating nonfiction, and more!

Puppy Parade

LEVEL **2**

GUIDED
READING
LEVEL **I**

This book is perfect for a **Progressing Reader** who:
- can figure out unknown words by using picture and context clues;
- can recognize beginning, middle, and ending sounds;
- can make and confirm predictions about what will happen in the text; and
- can distinguish between fiction and nonfiction.

Here are some **activities** you can do during and after reading this book:
- Make Connections: Every puppy in the parade wins a prize for something unique and wonderful about them. One puppy has the best ears, while another has the softest fur. Make prizes for your family and friends that tell them what you love about them!
- Homophones: Homophones are words that sound alike but have different meanings. In this book, the words *here* and *hear* are homophones. Think of homophones for these other words from the book: *tail, one, wear*. Then, on a separate piece of paper, write down each pair of homophones and a sentence that includes both words.

Remember, sharing the love of reading with a child is the best gift you can give!

—Bonnie Bader, EdM
  Penguin Young Readers program

*Penguin Young Readers are leveled by independent reviewers applying the standards developed by Irene Fountas and Gay Su Pinnell in *Matching Books to Readers: Using Leveled Books in Guided Reading*, Heinemann, 1999.

To Henry—JA

To Mack—DM

Penguin Young Readers
Published by the Penguin Group
Penguin Group (USA) Inc., 375 Hudson Street, New York, New York 10014, USA
Penguin Group (Canada), 90 Eglinton Avenue East, Suite 700, Toronto, Ontario M4P 2Y3, Canada
(a division of Pearson Penguin Canada Inc.)
Penguin Books Ltd, 80 Strand, London WC2R 0RL, England
Penguin Ireland, 25 St Stephen's Green, Dublin 2, Ireland (a division of Penguin Books Ltd)
Penguin Group (Australia), 707 Collins Street, Melbourne, Victoria 3008, Australia
(a division of Pearson Australia Group Pty Ltd)
Penguin Books India Pvt Ltd, 11 Community Centre, Panchsheel Park, New Delhi—110 017, India
Penguin Group (NZ), 67 Apollo Drive, Rosedale, Auckland 0632, New Zealand
(a division of Pearson New Zealand Ltd)
Penguin Books (South Africa), Rosebank Office Park, 181 Jan Smuts Avenue, Parktown North 2193, South Africa
Penguin China, B7 Jiaming Center, 27 East Third Ring Road North, Chaoyang District, Beijing 100020, China

Penguin Books Ltd, Registered Offices: 80 Strand, London WC2R 0RL, England

Text copyright © 2013 by Jill Abramson. Illustrations copyright © 2013 by Deborah Melmon.
All rights reserved. Published by Penguin Young Readers, an imprint of Penguin Group (USA) Inc.,
345 Hudson Street, New York, New York 10014. Manufactured in China.

Library of Congress Cataloging-in-Publication Data is available.

ISBN 978-0-448-45676-8 (pbk)   10 9 8 7 6 5 4 3 2 1
ISBN 978-0-448-46574-6 (hc)   10 9 8 7 6 5 4 3 2 1

PENGUIN YOUNG READERS

LEVEL 2

PROGRESSING READER

Puppy Parade

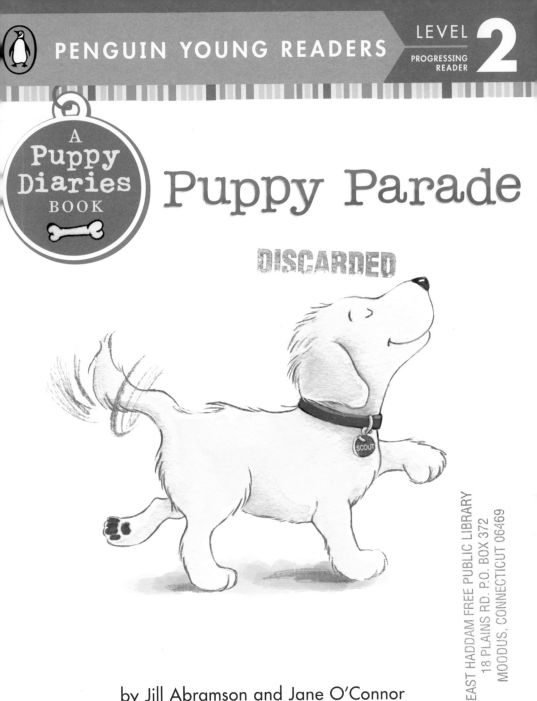

by Jill Abramson and Jane O'Connor
illustrated by Deborah Melmon

Penguin Young Readers
An Imprint of Penguin Group (USA) Inc.

Hello.

My name is Scout.

And this is Baby.

She is my best friend.

We are both puppies.

Only I am real and Baby isn't.

Today I get to march

in a puppy parade.

Baby wants to march, too.

But the parade is just for

real puppies.

We drive to town.

Baby has to stay in the car.

"Do not be sad," I tell her.

"I will be back soon."

Look at all the puppies!

At the end of the parade,

there will be prizes.

I have never won a prize.

I hope I win one today.

All the puppies line up.

The band starts playing.

We march down the street.

The puppy parade marches

past the bookstore.

A little boy points at me.

"Look at that cute puppy.

Her tail never stops wagging."

Maybe I will win the prize

for best tail.

The puppy parade marches

past the ice-cream store.

A little girl points at me.

"Look at that cute puppy.

See the way her ears stand up."

Maybe I will win the prize

for best ears.

The puppy parade stops

at the firehouse.

All the puppies get treats.

I let a little boy pet me.

"So soft," he says.

Maybe I will win the prize

for best fur.

We march all through town.

The puppy parade is over.

But I am not sad.

I am excited.

Now come the prizes!

Off I go!

Oops!

I slip and slide.

I land on my bottom

and spin around.

I try to get up.

But I fall down again.

I slip and slide and spin

all over again.

Everyone laughs.

"That puppy sure can dance!"

someone shouts.

I am a muddy mess.

I will not win the prize

for best tail.

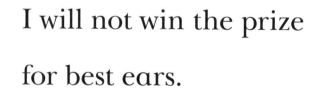

I will not win the prize

for best ears.

I will not win the prize

for best fur.

I will not win any prize!

I wish Baby were here.

Then I wouldn't feel so sad.

One by one, the prizes
are given out.
The prize for best tail
goes to a yellow puppy.
The prize for best ears
goes to a brown puppy.

The prize for best fur

goes to a puppy with black curls.

I am the only puppy

with no prize.

I want to go home!

Wait!

Did I just hear my name?

Yes!

I have won a prize.

It is for best dancer!

I am so proud.

I am so happy!

Baby is so happy, too.

And because she is my best
friend, I let her wear my prize
all the way home.